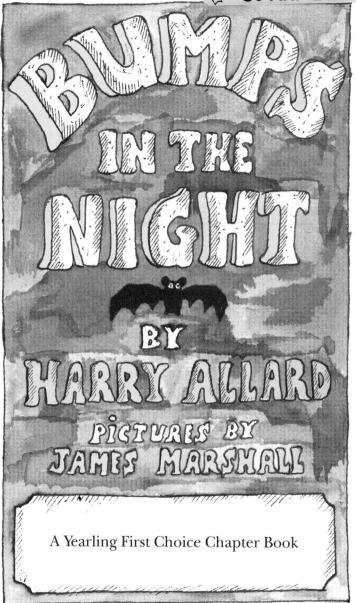

BUMPS IN THE NIGHT

BY HARRY ALLARD

PICTURES BY JAMES MARSHALL

A Yearling First Choice Chapter Book

For my niece *For my nephew*
Cathy Ann Dearolph *Alexander Christian Schwartz*
–H. A. –J. M.

Published by
Bantam Doubleday Dell Publishing Group, Inc.
1540 Broadway
New York, New York 10036
Published by arrangement with Doubleday
Text copyright © 1979 by Harry Allard
Illustrations copyright © 1979 by James Marshall

Library of Congress Cataloging-in-Publication Data
Allard, Harry.
  Bumps in the night / by Harry Allard; illustrated by James Marshall.
    p. cm.
  "A Yearling first choice chapter book."
  Summary: When he discovers his house is haunted, Dudley Stork enlists the help of his friends to find out what is causing the spooky noises.
  ISBN 0-385-32282-8 (alk. paper). —ISBN 0-440-41286-2 (pbk. : alk. paper)
  1. Animals—Fiction. [1. Ghosts—fiction. 2. Humorous stories.] I. Marshall, James, ill. II. Title.
PZ7.A413Bu 1996   96-3687 CIP AC
[E]—dc20

Hardcover: The trademark Delacorte Press® is registered in the U.S. Patent and Trademark Office and in other countries.

Paperback: The trademarks Yearling® and Dell® are registered in the U.S. Patent and Trademark Office and in other countries.

The text of this book is set in 17-point Baskerville.
Manufactured in the United States of America
October 1996

10 9 8 7 6 5 4 3 2 1

CONTENTS

1. A Sleepless Night   5

2. Trevor Hog Has an Idea   15

3. A Spooky Pair   23

4. The Séance   29

5. The Ghost   35

6. A New Friend   45

A SLEEPLESS NIGHT

Bong! Bong! Bong!

Bong! Bong! Bong!

Bong! Bong! Bong!

Bong! Bong! Bong!

The big grandfather clock in the hall
struck twelve: it was midnight.
But Dudley the Stork could not sleep.

He tossed and he turned.

He fluffed up his pillow.

He pulled his nightcap
down over his ears.

He counted sheep.

He counted white sheep.

He counted black sheep.

Then he counted spotted sheep.

But it did not work.

Dudley still could not get to sleep.

Outside, the wind was howling, howling,
and dark clouds
covered the pale moon.

Whoosh!

The big branches of an old elm tree
brushed against the side
of Dudley's house.
Somewhere in the dark
a hoot owl was hooting.
A shutter banged open and shut.
Windows rattled, floors creaked.

"What a night!" thought Dudley.
Then, suddenly, Dudley heard *IT*.

Bump! Bump! Bump!

"What a strange noise!"
said Dudley.
He turned on the light
next to his bed.
He put on his glasses.
Bump! Bump! Bump!

"It is too loud for a mouse,"
said Dudley,
"but it is too soft for an elephant."
Bump! Bump! Bump!

The bumping sound seemed
to be running up and down the stairs.
Now it was in the dining room.
Now it was in the den.

Whatever it was turned the TV on,
then turned the TV off.
"Odd!" Dudley muttered to himself.

Dudley got out of bed.
Putting on his bathrobe and slippers,
he peeked out the bedroom door
into the hall.

Bump! Bump! Bump!
The bumping sound was bumping
up the stairs again.

It was coming closer and CLOSER.

SMACK!
Something wet touched
Dudley's beak.

Dudley screamed and jumped
right out of his slippers.
His glasses fell off.
He slammed the bedroom door
shut and locked it.

He jumped into bed and
pulled the covers
over his head.

Dudley the Stork could not believe
what he had seen—
something big and white
running down the hall.

"This is a fine how-do-you-do!"
said Dudley.

"My lovely house is *haunted*!"

TREVOR HOG HAS AN IDEA

Early the next morning,
Dudley called
his best friend, Trevor Hog.

"Dudley, you sound worried,"
Trevor said.
"Is anything wrong?"
"Yes, Trevor, something is wrong,"
said Dudley.

"My house is haunted.
Things go bump in the night,
and something big and white
ran down the hall."

"It must have been a ghost,"
Trevor gulped.
"What can I do, Trevor?"
Dudley asked.

Trevor thought. He thought hard.
He twitched his ears
and wrinkled his nose.
"Hmm . . . hmm . . . ," he hummed.

At last Trevor cleared his throat
and said,
"Dudley, why don't you talk to the
ghost and find out what it wants?"

"Talk to a *ghost*?!" Dudley gasped.
"Why, I'd be too scared."

"But there are people
who can talk to ghosts,"
Trevor said.

"They are called mediums.
A medium acts as a go-between
between people and ghosts."
"Like a telephone operator?"
asked Dudley.

"Exactly," said Trevor.
"A medium puts you through
to ghosts . . . and other spooky things.

You must have a séance,"
Trevor continued.

"A *séance*?!" said Dudley.
"What on earth is a séance?"

"A séance," Trevor explained,
"is when a bunch of people sit around
a table at midnight with a medium."

"And what does the medium do?"
asked Dudley.
"The medium asks you
to hold hands," said Trevor.
"But why do you hold hands?"
asked Dudley.

"Is it because your hands are cold?"

"No, Dudley," Trevor said.

"Is it because you are passing
candy to one another?" Dudley asked.

"No, Dudley," Trevor said.

"Is it because you are all in love?"
Dudley asked.

"No, Dudley," Trevor said
in a low voice.

"It's because you're all so *scared*,
that's why, Dudley."

Dudley the Stork gulped.

By now it had stopped raining,
and there was no more
thunder or lightning.
Madam Kreepy and Lazlo
left as they had come, by taxi.

The next morning Dudley found that
Lazlo had forgotten Madam Kreepy's
small black bag.
Dudley looked inside it.
Besides Madam Kreepy's special hat,
he found two ham sandwiches,
a bag of gumdrops,
and a black and yellow yo-yo.

A NEW FRIEND

Donald the Horse proved
a charming friend.
He often visited Dudley and his
friends at night, because ghosts
can only go visiting at night.

Whenever Dudley the Stork
could not sleep, Donald would
drop in for a visit.

They would color pictures together
in a coloring book, or else Donald
would tell Dudley funny stories.

Donald helped Georgina make
a pretty pink party dress.
He made taffy for Grandpa Python
and fixed Grandpa's false teeth
when they broke chewing the taffy.
He helped Trevor with his arithmetic,
and he showed Dagmar the Baboon
how to dance a jig.

And from that time on,
no one was ever
scared again at night,
even when the wind howled,
and hoot owls hooted,
and doors banged open and shut,
and things went bump in the night.